MW01245352

# The Choir of Gravediggers

Mel Hall

# The Choir of Gravediggers

*The Choir of Gravediggers*
ISBN 978 1 76041 145 9
Copyright © Mel Hall 2016

First published 2016 by
GINNINDERRA PRESS
PO Box 3461 Port Adelaide 5015
www.ginninderrapress.com.au

'It by no means follows that because a man is a sexton, and constantly surrounded by the emblems of mortality, therefore he should be a morose and melancholy man; your undertakers are the merriest fellows in the world.'

Charles Dickens, from *The Story of the Goblins who stole a Sexton*

# 1

It wasn't exactly a fact you'd advertise, that you were born and raised in a cemetery. Life and death are meant to be separate, clearly opposed. But we were cemetery children, muddy-kneed, playing amongst graves.

The sky changed so quickly then – frosty pink to the ink-blot grey of a storm. Pillows of clouds you could sleep beneath, dark ones which sent you running for cover.

I recall the sound of hail on the roof, splitting on the pointed tower of our stone house, the cemetery lodge. My sister and I weren't allowed outside. We watched through rain-blurred windows as black umbrellas moved in slow procession, fine ice banking against mounds of graves.

Petals and whole flowers dropped from the sky when we weren't looking. If they landed on a grave, they turned to stone. And that's why the carved decorations of rose and ivy leaf looked so real.

The rain sang on the tin roof every few days – sun showers, storms at night. And water rose up from below, in underground streams. Our playground was often like a swamp, full of sunken stone crosses.

The dead sleep in their little damp abodes beneath the world of the living, waiting to rise again on Judgement day. It wasn't our business to be living there, skipping over burial plots, bouncing balls against crypts, playing hopscotch on paths between resting places. That's what people would say.

It wasn't our business to be muddying knees with the soil that separated the living and the dead.

*

The secrets of the cemetery were tucked under an old spring bed, in a small cottage at Lillydale. 1944; Germans had been interned, some preferring to gas themselves in kitchens rather than lose their dignity. There were rumours of Japanese helmets washing up on the shore at Darwin. But this room was unchanged, old and dusty as it had ever been.

After my mother died, I scraped open the louvre windows of her home, sunlight revealing a cosmos of floating dust. A dressmaker's model stood half-clad in a corner. Dutch milkmaids and porcelain clogs filled the sideboard of curios. I found strips of chiffon, lace, lemon satin, fabrics stuffed in strange places: crammed between tea and sugar canisters, in the bathroom cupboard, stacked beneath the laundry trough.

But it was under the single spring bed that I found it – what I've always searched for. The answers.

Why we ever lived there. Why my father, Charles Truelove, disappeared and later died. Why we left our graveyard home so suddenly, packed off to the middle of nowhere. Lillydale. And why we were told to never speak of St Kilda General Cemetery again.

A portrait of my father once hung proudly on the wall: his large round face, gentlemanly moustache, rosiness doctored into his cheeks. Now it lay flat under this bed, as though in a coffin. Under the bed were his framed certificates, engraved walking sticks, ribboned stacks of letters and hatboxes full of newspaper clippings. There were advertisements for Truelove's concerts, songs 'patriotic, sacred and nautical', his tours of Tasmania with the All Saints Boy Choristers, performances of his choir of gravediggers, Esprit de Corpse, notices of his music direction for the Masonic Lodges of Sorrow and moonlit performances for the Railway Musical Society.

But a greater number of the clippings were about the cemetery. The embezzlement, trafficking of graves, charges of bashing through coffins to make way for second burials. There were clippings about health tests, waterholes, the deaths of children from diphtheria blamed by the closeness of graves to their homes. There were admit-one passes to the Truelove Defence Fund concert, circulars signed 'Hubert Tope and Nathaniel Dear', convicted grave-robbers, who accused my dad of even greater evils. I found notices of his disappearance, his three trials for embezzlement – the first two juries being unable to decide on his fate. There was a notice when he later filed for insolvency, and another when he died of a singing-induced heart attack aged fifty-nine.

After he died, my mother's wedding ring disappeared from her finger. She wore it on a necklace, which she kept tucked under her blouse. She looked very uncomfortable if any person ever saw it.

I never realised until she died that my father had kept everything. Threatening letters slipped under doors, correspondences with Detective Walker, who helped him catch the 'resurrection men' (men who made a living from the anatomy of stolen dead) personal files, notes, ledgers. Facts. He even kept journals, and had printed a letter for private circulation in his defence, explaining the whole matter, all the matters, in depth.

Now I could jot down all the facts I've learnt, and the list of truths would number in the hundreds. But I think this would make me forget what I even wanted to ask.

Now I know my questions – I have collected them, given them the shape, almost, of real objects. And to answer them, I need to start at the very beginning.

# 2

Even his name was theatrical: Charles 'St George' Truelove. He addressed the world with open arms, and the puffed-up chest of an opera singer. When meeting a crowd as small as three, he would remove his top hat, bow, kiss hands and respond to small pleasantries with bellowing laughter. The movement of his body and his silent gestures conveyed presence, personality. His smallest comments commanded attention – it was all about his tone and smiling eyes. A simple question like 'How are you?' seemed like an announcement, warranting an exclamation for a reply.

His face was round and white like the moon. I remember it rising above my covers after he knelt to say goodnight. He sang me a song about the big face high in the sky, telling all the children it was time for bed. And I thought my father was the moon, or at least a close relative.

But I also believed he was part elephant. Elephants were his favourite animal, and he had a special walking stick made, with a miniature elephant on the handle. You curled three fingers under its belly, and tucked your index finger under the trunk to hold a firm grip. He would go on all fours and give me elephant-back rides, I imagined his moustache as a pair of tusks. His laughter was so loud, it might have erupted from a trunk.

In all, I believed my father was a magical creature, a wizard and a shape-shifter. His baton was really a wand. When he conducted, he was gathering the force of spirits to help cast a spell. He was Moses, commanding the Red Sea to separate, creating a dry ocean path for the Israelites. I remember the overwhelming sound of singing, the congregation rising like tall waves, heads bobbing above me, while I was stuck on the ocean floor.

He didn't belong in the cemetery. He adored the opulence of fashion, the absurd frilliness of ladies' collars. He was fascinated by whirring inventions, and thrived on the excitement of performing encores to eager crowds. He loved the music of Gilbert and Sullivan, the comic operas of

Offenbach, tales of far-away lands now under British dominion. He was loud and gregarious, a master of witty and dramatic rebukes. He was a people-person, not a dead-people-person.

I often wonder which parts of him were his alone, and which were defined by the age. Some people never knew the cruelty of war. They were soaked in optimism, supremely confident in exploration and invention. In this relentless sanguinity, the sombre nature of death could be masked, disguised by ornate headstones, floral arrangements and singing gravediggers. Mourners could be cheated of their right to proper grief – that brief moment of madness in the soul.

\*

His life has an implausible, fairy-tale quality to it. Growing up in Somerstown, London, he was a child chorister at St Pancras Old Church. But, in his words, he was 'destined for a greater purpose'. He wasn't kidnapped, like one of the child-performers for the Royal circuses in the Middle Ages. It was all above board; his parents agreed, and he went to live in Windsor to sing in the choir at St George's Royal Chapel. He was schooled there also, learning the artful skill of curling clef signs, and to write in his unimpeachable copperplate script. His days began with prayers and vocal warm-ups, and ended with evensong.

He claimed to have sung for Queen Victoria herself, and was allowed a boiled sweet from her imperial lolly tin. He always kept a portrait of her on the wall, and often spoke fondly of the monarch. He insisted that imperial sweets tasted much better than regular ones, and that we should always aspire to greater things. When her majesty died, he held a special concert in her honour, choosing from a repertoire of songs composed about the sovereign, such as Stainer's 'Flora Queen', Sir George Martin's 'The seaboards are her mantle's hem', and other popular titles: 'Lady on a Silver Throne', 'To her beneath whose steadfast star', 'With still increasing blessings', 'A Century's Penultimate', and 'With wisdom, goodness and grace'. I was left with the understanding that she and my father had been on very close terms.

After leaving school, my father began an apprenticeship with an undertaker. He apparently taught his fellow coffin-carvers to sing, so that hymns, glees and part-songs were often heard floating from the workshop. The stride of people passing was often quickened at the eerie sound.

He always harboured a secret wish to become a professional singer. However, there weren't many employment opportunities for British musicians in England at the time. Italians and Germans were preferred for operas, both comic and serious.

Disillusioned British performers travelled to Australia, seeking their fortune in unmusical ventures such as gold-panning and settling land. But with a dearth of professional musicians, even in Marvellous Melbourne, many stumbled upon fame as conductors of local choirs. There were few instrumental bands, but amateur choral societies seemed to go forth and multiply the way followers of Jesus did all those years ago.

And so my father fitted into a trend. He didn't emigrate to Australia to make music, but ended up doing so, as if by accident.

He came from England to sell funeral accessories at the Melbourne International Exhibition of 1880–81. He told swashbuckling tales of the eventful passage; a shipwreck off the African coast, and how he salvaged his consignment of stock from a near-watery death. Everywhere there were coffins bobbing about in the sea. Luckily, many were saved, and the full complement of elaborate ceramic grave decorations was left unscathed.

He greatly enjoyed his time at the Exhibition. I always thought this suited him; my father was the definition of an exhibitionist. And he was born in 1851, the year of the Crystal Palace Exhibition in London.

He remembered the Melbourne Exhibition with the wonderment of a child. It was like a giant curiosity shop. Several annexes were required for the event – not even the vast Exhibition Building could contain the realised dreams of so many men. Extensive displays of Belgian glassware sat opposite Italian statuary, arranged in military-like columns. South Australia contributed a bush scene, complete with replica natives and mini-fauna. France boasted finds from colonies in Algeria, while Western Australia displayed huge shells which retained the sound of the ocean.

My father spoke of horse stables, billiard tables and bell pulls with faces like gargoyles. The full scope of a hatter's emporium was packed in glass cabinets – bowling hats floating on the heads of invisible gentlemen. Fingerprints of children were pressed on the glass as they watched in awe, wondering what magical spell suspended the hats in mid-air.

There was Icelandic moss, mosaic flooring, Chubb's collection of patent safes, spades and shovels, pliers and pincers, screw-cutters and wrenches, celluloid jewellery, collars and cuffs, impasto salad bowls, cruets and butter dishes, fourteen-horsepower portable steam engines, tapioca, model Micronesian proas, India rubber, fluid magnesia and Florida water. He purchased, from the Worcester Royal Porcelain Company, a drinking cup made in the shape of an elephant's trunk.

During his stay in Melbourne, my father took interest in many church and musical activities. He became the voice-trainer for the choir at All Saints' Church, situated near his cheap lodgings on Chapel Street in East St Kilda. This came about through a close friendship with the minister of the church, Father Gregory, a man with bright and intense eyes. I'd say they even resembled my father's own.

Gregory believed that the more intricate the ornamentation of a church, the deeper a person could be led into spiritual contemplation. He was a proud Tractarian, a rebel in the Diocese of Melbourne, which viewed excessive symbolism and adornment as suspiciously Catholic. Forever the radical, Father Gregory created a church so ornate it resembled a concise version of the Arts and Crafts movement. Unfortunately, he sent All Saints' Church bankrupt in the process, and pew rents were required to cover the debt for years to come. People did chip in: some paid for fittings, others added finishing touches to the stencilled chancel decorations, and women embroidered biblical symbols on the prayer cushions. Gregory would later leave Melbourne due to financial difficulties. Father would describe watching his ship leave the docks until it became a mere speck in the ocean's great eye.

My father also kept many of Gregory's books. The majority of his theological and general library was sold off by the auctioneers Gemmell Tuckett & Co., but he donated a sundry selection to my father; Plumptre's *Lazarus and other Poems, David Copperfield*, J.S. Mill's *Representative Government*, Flamank's *Mind and Matter, Commonsense Management of the Stomach, Memoirs of Wordsworth*, Coleridge's *Aids to Reflection, Clerical*

*Elocution*, Bishop Skinner's *Scottish Episcopacy*, Charles Dickens's *Child's History of England*, titles on artists in Egypt, moral philosophy and ancient history. Each book was treasured.

During his stay, father also performed in the chorus of Offenbach's latest comic opera, *La fille du Tambour major*, travelling throughout Melbourne, even performing at the Opera House.

When that tour finished, he volunteered to create a music library, and managed all the sheet music required for the Australian Musical Union Festival. He administered many rehearsals, choral and instrumental, keeping detailed ledgers of items on loan. He performed this menial job, I assume, just for the sake of being around music. As a reward, my father was presented with a handsome diamond locket.

The Musical Union was castigated by music writer for *The Argus*, Figaro, for paying Mr Charles Truelove so well. A union representative replied, and a detailed account of the tasks performed by my father was published in the newspaper. Early on, my father achieved a small fraction of fame – or notoriety.

Soon enough, his two years had expired, and he was due to return to England. But my father was made two handsome offers. First, he was promoted to choirmaster at All Saints' Church.

Also, Father Gregory had recommended he apply for the position of manager at St Kilda General Cemetery, only half a mile from the church down Dandenong Road. From one hundred and forty applicants he was successful, and that was how he came to live at the cemetery lodge, a large two-storey stone house, with a small pointed tower on the eastern side.

Many people were critical of my father's appointment, since he had no relevant cemetery experience. Rude rumours began to circulate early on. People claimed he was a mere sexton – a puppet of the church, singing and burying the dead when required.

\*

My father was good at his job. From the start, he had a plan to improve the cemetery, and initially he succeeded.

When he began, the cemetery was just a plot of bush. Nobody wanted to be buried there. When graves were dug, snakes were routinely found, then killed and cut up with sharp-edged spades. Occasionally a mouse, furry and wet with eyes closed, would drop from a leathery segment of dead snake.

There was also a large amount of water seeping up from underground, sinking in from the hills. Father had concrete foundations built under the cemetery walls, some reaching down fifteen feet, to prevent the flood waters from further corrupting graves. The water was kept out, apart from four 'waterholes', as my father called them. Natural wells. He planted shinus motley and pinus insignus trees to mark these spots, and they were avoided as burial plots.

Cement kerbing was placed around paths through the cemetery, making clearer the distinctions between Roman Catholic, Jewish, Methodist, and Church of England routes to heaven. Railings were placed around the graves, to minimise the risk of people tripping and falling six feet. The same railing was used as a proxy picket fence for the cemetery lodge. This was cheaper than any alternative, but it implied the unfortunate comparison of our backyard to a burial plot.

Father also began to clear the bush. As part of a cemetery beautification plan, he planted palms, cycads, crotons, pelargonium, caladium, rhododendron, azaleas, one and two leaf cape tulips from South Africa and oriental species from the East Indies.

He built a conservatory, affectionately called Crystal Palace, and there operated an on-site florist and nursery. The cemetery became a veritable tropical resort. A local photographer took shots of the graveyard paradise, and an orange-skied cemetery was featured in a postcard series depicting Marvellous Melbourne.

I can't be sure whether the beautification project was the reason for the vast increase in cemetery funds. There was also the choir of gravediggers.

When my father first took up the cemetery, he was notified of an ongoing problem with grave-robbing. Bartholomew Hope, a grave-decorator who worked opposite the cemetery grounds on Dandenong Road, informed my father that the resident gravediggers were responsible for the sacrilegious acts. So from the beginning, Father welcomed his new employees with great suspicion, and set about devising ways to catch them out.

One Sunday after church at All Saints', he met a fellow parishioner named Mr Walker, a retired policeman who took on cases of private detection as a hobby. After a sobering discussion of the unsavoury crimes, they formulated a plan of attack. Walker would sleep on a downstairs couch, while Father sat upstairs on lookout, watching for the criminals. Walker arranged a pulley-based contraption (basically, a bell on a string). Father would pull it, the bell would ring close to Walker's ear, and he would be able to dash outside and catch the criminals.

Armed with binoculars, Father thrice saw owls perch and hoot on the blue-grey headstones. He did this many nights, for about two weeks. And then one night, not long past midnight, they appeared: a band of men carrying a large grey blanketed thing, which might have been a plank of wood. One man held a single lantern. It swayed near his face, and the crooked jaw of Bartholomew Hope himself was illuminated. He had presented my father the false lead to cover his own tracks. One man had a wooden shovel – capable of digging without producing noise – cast over his shoulder.

In shock at this betrayal of trust, Father rang the bell hurriedly. Walker jumped to attention, dashed outside and caught them in the act.

The men offered bribes, but Detective Walker and my father declined. The grave-robbers were tried and found guilty. Instead of receiving a prison sentence, the men were dealt hefty fines, but permitted to conduct business as usual across the road from the cemetery.

My father felt very sorry for casting accusing eyes on his own gravediggers. As a treat, he took them all for a drink at a local hotel, and it turned into a merry night of song. Some of the big-shouldered men, with their large curled moustaches and muddied aprons, had voices sweet and low.

Half in jest, my father put forth the notion of a choir named Esprit de Corpse. Singing gravediggers evidently had high morale, but the saying could also take an alternative meaning: 'joy of the dead'.

The choir quickly became a huge success. They practised twice a week at the cemetery lodge, but apparently their voices could be heard daily, melodies floating over the graves.

Father had a special programme printed. Funeral-goers could select from a long repertoire; seafaring tunes for sailors, military march songs for soldiers, and ballads expressing nostalgia for the mother country. The list was constantly updated and amended. Rumours of the choir spread, and people came specifically to request the favourite song of their beloved deceased.

# 3

Back then, there was singing everywhere, all the time – singing in the streets, in rented town halls, in churches during the evening.

Most people learned the solfege method of reading music in schools and churches. Schoolchildren would sing in unison, accompanying do re mis with strange hand signals. Far more readable than staff notation, the method was a means for the pleasures of written music to be extended to every man. Along with fervent members of the temperance movement, the railways workers had their own choral societies, there were community women's choirs, and choirs specialising in drinking and party songs.

E.W. Cole, the main music shop on Bourke Street and specialist in printed music, was constantly running out of stock. Jolly round-bellied men, women in complicated skirts, even children would come in and peruse the sheets. They would inspect the sheet-music for madrigals like Danby's 'Awake Aeolian Lyre', Gastoldi's 'Soldiers Brave and Gallant Be', or humorous pieces like 'The Torpedo and the Whale' from the comic opera *Olivette*. And with the ability to read both horizontally and vertically, they would sing the tune to themselves, and decide whether they liked the sound.

A gramophone permanently sat outside Mr Cole's shop window. Dramatic overtures mingled with horse-clops and the murmured sounds of strangers greeting. Signs reading, 'Offenbach's latest, in store now!', would draw in a crowd, recordings and sheet music disappearing instantly.

Around the time of Federation, it was patriotic songs like 'The Absent Minded Beggar' that captured people's imaginations. Arthur Sullivan's popular song stood for the Boer War, the glory of fighting for Britain. Mr Cole, and many other vendors, also sold 'Absent Minded Beggar' memorabilia. The heroic 'gentleman in khaki' was stamped on matchstrikers, cigar cases and postcards. In 1900, my father held a series of patriotic concerts around Melbourne. This song always required an encore, and the buildings were always full.

The singing was pandemic, an infectious disease. It was only a matter of time before the choir fever reached those burying the dead.

Why did they sing so much? I've always wondered. There was a shortage of instruments and music teachers in the colonies, I know that. Singing was the next-best option to the violin or piano. But singing really suited the age – the era of confidence, optimism, of strong belief in causes. Singing was a way of making a clear proclamation.

The Great War changed everything. But my father never knew how the world became misshapen. He died long before Crystal Palace in London was destroyed by fire, or the grandiose Melbourne Exhibition Building became a lonely place, a mere vestige of a happier past. My school exams were held there. Two sparrows flew about the dusty glass windows, unaware of their own irreverence.

*

Now I have told one part of the story. But it doesn't explain how I came to exist. My father found romance in the colonies.

But to tell that story, I need to go back to another choirmaster in Melbourne at the time. His name was George Arthur Broadbent, but many knew him as 'the Rechabite on a penny-farthing'. And he was my grandfather.

# 4

Grandfather Broadbent was like King Midas, except everything he touched turned to song. After dinner parties spent in silence, he would often be asked to sing. Somehow, he managed to coax sound from everyone else present. Whether with written music or without, he would have a party singing a round, part-song, catch, canon or glee.

Although a man of a holy kind of spirit, a member of the Temperance Society, he liked the cheekiness of Henry Purcell. Jovial friends laughed after singing catches like 'The London Constable'. The song told the story of an alleged policeman with a 'noddle-full of Ale', caught out and placed in front of a midnight magistrate, in his 'wooden chair of State', all because he stayed out late drinking and his wife locked him out. Initially, the magistrate thought the drunkard was a Latin-speaking 'Mohametan' – a dangerous man. But the constable convinced the magistrate that he was a civil man, an honest Tory, and was allowed to bounce 'light the gentleman home'.

Broadbent taught all his children about harmony and counterpoint at an early age. He helped them to write small poems, then sing them to the simple tunes like 'Frère Jacques'. The lyrics to a popular round my mother taught me were 'I see bees buzzing round making lots of honey eat with bread.'

I never knew Grandfather Broadbent, except through the poems and songs. He died long before I was born.

I found later that he instigated the Floral and Choral festivals. The Melbourne Town Hall was rented for a weekend in spring. Plumage bobbed about on women's hats as they sipped small cups of tea, inspecting displays of chrysanthemum bunches, elaborate tropical arrangements and garlands of roses.

Broadbent led the Band of Hope – the musical wing of the temperance movement, However, due to the shortage of instrumentalists in colonial Melbourne, the band consisted of a piano, a drum, and a large group of zealous Rechabite singers.

They sang whilst men and women bought flowers, soaking up the sense of good moral hygiene. At the Sunday's close, cuttings, parched leaves, petals and prickles were swept from the floor. For days afterwards, the hall smelt fresh and new, a baptism of the air.

I now know that Broadbent saw a deeper connection than the rhyme – floral and choral. But then he saw connections in everything, amongst all things. Flowers sing, if you listen closely. Also in singing, you can document the sound of a particular flower. This didn't mean that different varieties translated as different notes. Colours, shades of pink and blue, had corresponding tones – some deep and full, others thin and crisp, some wavering on the cusp of two worlds.

He would contemplate the details of veins in a leaf, and in doing so find greater clarity in his own being. It was the liquidity of the Spirit, he believed. In the crisp air of the garden, he would fill his cup, drinking up the holiness of nature. Then his singing was liquid too, an overflowing. Tears came, because the sound produced by singing could not contain all his feeling: his overwhelming gratitude for the presence of God.

But then everything in life was liquid. As a tailor, Grandfather Broadbent talked about folds in the cloth resembling water, or the flowing landscape. He had an uncanny ability to create apparently seamless garments, clothing so perfect it seemed to have grown from the earth. And as he folded, sewed, he would sing notes crisp and clear.

A tall thin man with pointed nose, ears, beard and shoes, he seemed permanently perched upon his penny-farthing bicycle, a top hat perched upon his head. When he stepped from his seat on high, it seemed he was descending clumsily from the clouds.

He helped found the Good Roads Movement, championing the right to smooth and safe paths, because he believed that 'the good road leads to heaven'. His whole family followed him on safety bicycles to church each Sunday. The family of cyclists seemed to glide like swans, mother and father followed by cygnets in silent unison.

It was always Broadbent's mission to create heaven on earth. In 1887, people said he came close to achieving this end. It was the year of Queen Victoria's Golden Jubilee. Leading up to June, he rode all over the Anglican diocese of Melbourne on that penny-farthing, his son following him on a tricycle with a crate full of sheet music. Every day of the week, he made visitations to Sunday-scholars of parishes small and large. He taught each group a suite of songs, both patriotic and sacred. Instructions and sheet music were left with choirmasters.

And this is how my grandfather, George Arthur Broadbent, came to meet my father, Charles Truelove. Sheet music, and a stack of neatly pressed multicoloured flags were distributed to the children at All Saints' Church in St Kilda. As the resident choirmaster, Truelove was given a long list of instructions. The impromptu choir, consisting of the regular group of boy-choristers, and a flock of three dozen Sunday-scholars, practised every Sunday after church.

The culmination of all Broadbent's hard work came on 24 June 1887. Before then, every choirmaster, enthusiastic parent and chorister only witnessed a snippet of the grand plan. It was like a verse from the book of Corinthians: 'we first see dimly then face to face, now I know in part, but then I will know in full'. Broadbent was planning a garment beyond belief in size and splendour, nobody had seen more than an inch-by-inch square of fabric.

There were too many performers to fit on any conventional stage, some twenty-five thousand Sunday-scholars and junior choristers in total. Instead, they took up the entire eastern side of the Exhibition Building's great hall. Sunlight shone behind the figures so they appeared luminescent, like heavenly presences. As well as singers, there were three community brass brands, pianos, and a grand organ – all played by friends of George, believers in the master-designer.

It could have been a disaster. Many audience members felt an attack of nerves in the silence before the first sounds, dreading the embarrassment for the conductor when an eruption of noisy disunity broke upon the majestic hall. But Broadbent never believed it was possible to fail, and so he didn't.

He did not use conducting batons, but instead flags, each chorister apparently responding to a single flutter. My father described the way the performers followed, waving flags back at their conductor, as 'dutifully, beautifully'.

They sang a combination of hymns in four-part harmony: 'All Things Bright and Beautiful', 'Be Thou My Vision', 'For all the Saints', 'Rock of the Ages', 'Guide Me O Thou Great Redeemer', and patriotic anthems such as 'God Save the Queen' and 'Jerusalem at my Feet'.

The singing brought tears to the eyes, even of the most unimpressionable persons present. Proud parents grasped at each other's hands; women and men wept into handkerchiefs. Many of the children looked bewildered at first, stunned by the sudden waterfalls of sound cascading around them.

They received a standing ovation and gave three encores.

After the performance, Father sought out Broadbent. However, the conductor was not able to descend from his rostrum for some time. He was encircled by an enthusiastic crowd, much like a queen bee surrounded by drones.

Off to the side, my father noticed a small group of women packing flags into large trunks. He offered a hand and they accepted graciously. Father noticed as he rolled, how perfect, seamless and silken each flag appeared. Two of the ladies smiled, and continued to furl in silence. These women were Broadbent's wife and daughter – my mother and grandmother.

My father always said how serendipitous it was, meeting my mother at the Great Hall. After recounting tales of all the treasures of the Melbourne Exhibition, the wonders of the world he was surrounded by on a daily basis, he said that none of these even began to compare with our mother's eyes: icy blue, like frosty clouds. They barely exchanged words, but her eyes spoke of eternity.

And she was a good luck charm. The following year, 1888, Father tried his hand at competitive flower arranging. His work was displayed in a horticultural show in the Avenue of Nations, beneath the northern dome of the Great Hall. He won awards for his collections of pansies (fancy), cut flowers and verbenas.

Amongst the rich variegated blossoms and delicious perfumes of flowers, he thought of my mother, retracing his steps to exactly where they had met. He had a vision of their wedding, the scent of her rose bouquet and milk white skin.

We often heard stories about the circumstances of their meeting. But the one detail my parents missed was the fact of the gold band on my mother's wedding finger. My mother was already married. Perhaps my father noticed the ring and felt for a moment that the gates of heaven were closed to him.

*

As years passed, the fame of Esprit de Corpse increased. My father's choir of gravediggers would have preceded his name – if it weren't for the fact that his name was so memorable itself. But then, his All Saints Boys Choir also made him an eminent figure in the Melbourne music scene. He held concerts throughout the city, organised charity events at hospitals and regularly toured through regional Victoria and Tasmania.

On Sundays, people came to church just for the music, the theatrics of it all. The one thousand seats of All Saints' Church were routinely filled. People said it was as good as the opera. He was called the 'Napoleon of Choirmasters'.

But it was the story of the choir of gravediggers that led Grandfather Broadbent to purchase a plot at this particular cemetery. It was the thought of being surrounded by music in death.

In contemplating his own end long before he knew of any illness, he courteously considered his wife. Broadbent decided St Kilda would not be too far for her to travel from her South Yarra home on Sundays. Every Sabbath she would lay a bouquet of flowers on his grave, flowers from seeds planted by her departed husband. He also let her know, long in advance, what he wanted on the epitaph: 'we will come to him in singing'. And when he did finally die, in 1896, it was not only Esprit de Corpse who sang at the funeral. Rechabites from the Temperance Society proudly sang of abstinence, several ex-Sunday-scholars performed parts memorised from childhood, and enthusiasts from the Floral and Choral Festival joined in on their favourite hymns. There were several hundred people at the cemetery and, as I'm told, it was a fine day. There was joviality and laughter; they came to him in singing.

And this is how my mother and father came to meet for the second time. This time, there was no wedding band on her finger. And they were married within the year.

# 5

My mother was a good Samaritan. People would always comment on her kindness. When I think of her, I recall ironed pillowcases, the smell of soap, Epp's cocoa for breakfast on Sundays, Steedman's soothing mixture for colds and coughs, the scent of oranges, pots of fig jam bubbling away on the stove, the smell of fresh bread rising, wafting through our home with great promise. I remember her brushing, plaiting and braiding my hair. She seemed to untangle knots just by the touch of her hand. I remember her as a particular constellation of comforts.

In the waxy morning light, I would tiptoe downstairs and find her at work with needle and thread – mending clothes, attaching buttons, embroidering. She never sang very loudly, but on those mornings, I would press my face to the cool banister and listen for her voice. Later in the day, when the house was more alive, she would sit at her Singer sewing machine. It hit a tuneful, creaking note as she pressed foot upon pedal, and this was her music.

She was quiet and even-tempered. Actually, I don't remember a time when she wasn't smiling, in her gentle and honest way. I wouldn't say she was always happy or vivacious. She was just calm, content. It seemed she had the perfect temperament for the death industries.

As a sort of wedding gift, my father opened a company called Adamant Monumental Works across the road from the cemetery. He left it in my mother's charge. A second nursery, the Sunbeam, was also added to these premises. She employed her father's Scottish cousin, another dedicated Rechabite, to manage Adamant, and several other cousins and friends to work with her.

*

My sister was born first, in 1897. I was born the year after.

My earliest memories are of the music in our house. It always seemed to have a drifting quality, to hover in the air like a ghostly presence. Music wafted up the stairs from the gramophone – a crackling rendition of Handel's *Messiah*, or 'Tit Willow' from *The Mikado*. Then there was the choir singing around the piano, my father somehow accompanying and conducting at the same time. At church on Sundays, I could almost drown in the sound, the choirs of angels singing in exaltation.

I remember often lying in bed at night and hearing a choir. I thought I saw them, in their cassocks and surplices, led by a man carrying an unwieldy cross, wandering about the graveyard and blessing the dead. I never knew if this choir was real, in my dreams or my imagination. I often convinced myself, this was the music of ghosts.

And then I remember the man in the photograph.

The image takes over in my mind. It was almost comic. Evidently taken in a photographic studio, the background was dark as a night sky, but his face was lit up so his eyes were clear and bright as stars. He leant against a pitchfork, a bale of hay next to him, straw scattered on the ground. Smiling in a wide-eyed way, he seemed about to burst into laughter. I often wondered if the photograph captured a private joke shared with someone outside the camera's view.

The studio was attempting to disguise itself as a 'farm scene', but this was contradicted by the fine suit the man wore. Though he did have the wholesome look of a man who worked the land, the suit just didn't make sense. If only he'd been wearing some trousers held up with suspenders and a soiled shirt. He had black hair, a black curled moustache and his eyes seemed deep and dark. He was almost frightening. But the strangest thing was, no one ever talked about him. A few times I remember my father found me staring at the man, and it was as if he pretended not to have seen me.

The photograph sat to the left side of the mantelpiece at the cemetery lodge. There were no other portraits taking pride of place on this ledge. This space was instead taken up by potted flowers, floral wallpaper behind it.

I often saw my mother gazing at the picture, and remember she smiled, but with sad eyes. Sometimes she rested a hand on her chest, grasping at an invisible necklace. I swear I caught her quietly laughing at the photograph once. I don't remember hearing her laugh apart from that.

I had a half-brother then, Ralph. He addressed my father politely as Mr Truelove. Ralph didn't live with us; being quite a bit older, he took lodgings close by on Chapel Street and worked at Adamant. I remember him staring at the photograph as well. But like everybody else, he never spoke about it.

Only once, I remember my sister said in a teasing way, 'He's a wizard. He disappeared, and we are all waiting for him to come back.'

I never took what she said seriously, she had obviously drawn from the story of Christ's second coming.

I don't know why I have such a strong memory of the photograph. It was just a small thing, but it was mysterious. An irregularity. And I think that's what we remember – the things that stick out like sore thumbs.

# 6

For a time, life was truly perfect. But maybe that's just what we believe as children. We think the world is a safe and happy place.

I'm not sure when it all started to go wrong. It was more like a series of small signs than any noticeably apocalyptic event.

One day a grave was reopened, as a man wanted to be buried alongside his wife. This was usually easy. A hole was dug, coffin exhumed, the hole widened slightly, and coffins replaced. But this day, the gravedigger found the hole was half-filled with water, like one of the natural wells. The coffin was floating, and suddenly my father's shipwreck all those years ago seemed like a bad omen.

The gravedigger fetched my father, and some other men swarmed around to watch. They opened the lid and found the body had turned upside down, floating, as if having drowned in the water.

Another day, it was the funeral of a society man. The hole was dug, and even before a depth of six foot was reached, water began to seep up from the dirt. It became a case of digging through mud. Pails of water were retrieved, but it kept magically reappearing.

There was no disguising the fact from the funeral attendees. It was raining. My father tried to keep up the dignified image. He stood, solemn, with his extra-tall top hat and tails coat, gloved hands held respectfully together. The singing gravediggers couldn't disguise the slight splash as the coffin was lowered into the grave.

A respected Justice of the Peace said to him on leaving, 'Damn you, Truelove, you're burying my friend in a waterhole.'

And that would have really hurt my father, who always strived to be considered a true gentleman.

Also, the cemetery was becoming overcrowded. Paths between graves were becoming increasingly crooked. More than once, my father found a widow lost. After laying a wreath on her husband's grave, she turned to find the path on which she'd arrived had disappeared. Not wanting to risk the sacrilegious act of treading on graves, the women began to call out in despair. My father would assist them back, manoeuvring their way along the dirt paths as though negotiating a tight mountain passage.

Then there was the bad publicity. A local doctor, Charles Bage, was writing regular letters to the editor of *The Argus*, claiming the cemetery should be closed. He claimed it was unsanitary for the graveyard to be situated so close to people's homes.

My father wrote back in defence, 'Look at my children! I would parade them as exemplars of the fine sanitary conditions of this cemetery!' He also reminded the public that the cemetery had pride of place long before the domestic residents. These homes had sprung up quite recently in the scheme of things.

Also, the local stonemason and former grave-robber, Bartholomew Hope began to publish a circular titled 'The TRUTH about St Kilda Cemetery!' In it, he claimed that the burial costs were so high because cemetery funds were being poured into unnecessary beautification, in service of Truelove's lavish tastes. Hope criticised my father for using the official St Kilda Cemetery Coach, with the full regalia of red-tasselled horses, as transport to any manner of social events: picnics, weddings, meetings, parties. He would arrive and step out with his trademark operatic open arms, as if he was the main event.

My father defended himself on this point also. He was advertising the St Kilda General Cemetery at such events, assuring that his organisation had a strong community presence.

But the most disturbing event of all was the day Crystal Palace Nursery was torn down. My father believed Mr Hope engineered this event. He claimed my father was profiteering from death. His close position to the graves meant he had an unfair business advantage – other florists were going under. And Hope had a case.

The building was reduced to rubble within the hour. For months, my father mourned the cheap selling-off of his chrysanthemum bunches at church fetes. If there ever was an omen, it was this.

From this time forth, there was always a measure of my father that was unknowable. There was bellowing laughter, charming jokes, bear hugs I wished would last a lifetime. But then there were his 'bouts of illness', his 'fits of the mind'.

All I knew was that the bedroom door stayed closed, opened intermittently as a silver tray of eggs and toast, or sandwiches and tea were taken in. I sneaked a look once, saw the great round curve of his body under the covers. It shuddered slightly, and I couldn't look again.

*

It was 1905, and I was seven when he disappeared. I walked downstairs and saw the empty space on the hat stand. Only a small space, but empty all the same, carved and set like a question mark in time. It was just the first stage in a process of vanishing.

The day before, he had been asked to step down as cemetery manager. He, and the trustees, were accused of trafficking in graves and embezzlement of funds. They were apparently selling graves to themselves at a cheap rate, and then re-selling them at a very profitable price.

My father denied all knowledge of this, and the trustees did the same. It became a case of how many fingers were pointed at whom. Mr Charles Truelove was outnumbered.

His disappearance made things much worse. Mr Hope and company rallied outside the cemetery, shouting and laughing, with placards reading, 'The horse has bolted!'

My mother, in her mild-tempered version of a nervous wreck, sought help from the police. The crowd moved on.

The now very elderly Detective Walker offered assistance in finding my father. After just a few days of expert detection, he found that Truelove had packed a few belongings and was nowhere to be found.

One of the trustees, Mr Elmslie, came to our house days after the disappearance. He had found a note slipped under the door. It wasn't Truelove's usual perfectly curled handwriting script, but was quite messy. It made my mother suspicious that he had not even written the words.

The note read, 'I am disappearing from the haunts of man, and I shall not return until you clear my name.'

Several months later, my mother received a letter postmarked Bournemouth, England. My father explained, in a script which indicated a clearer frame of mind, that he was having a moment of illness when he left. He had somehow forgotten the last twenty-five years, and felt suddenly pressed to return to England. He was staying at Bournemouth to avoid the cold. He was busying himself with church activities and enjoying early morning walks through the Pleasure Gardens and Victorian Folly.

My mother felt terrible for him. The church had gathered together a donation of ten pounds to the Truelove family. My mother sent most of this sum to him. She understood, she always understood.

*

I am not sure why I write any more. It's a kind of plea, I guess. I need to know in full.

My sister didn't need such clarity. To her, the contents of these hatboxes – the secrets – would simply serve as Truelove memorabilia. She would gather them up and create a shrine to him. She would frame his certificates for first-class verbenas and performances to sick children. His ivory elephant walking stick would be repaired and hung above the mantelpiece. His round face would shine down on her children, perpetuating the myth that he was the moon. These were pieces of a man which spoke clearly of the whole.

In her gushy reverence for him, my sister worked hard to become a champion flower arranger, winning awards at several horticultural shows. It was always about the flowers. I really think I've had enough to last a lifetime. If a man ever bought me flowers, it would disturb me.

It wasn't the same for her. She married a pianist she met at a dance hall, the kind who learns by ear and plays songs perfectly in the wrong key. It was a bunch of wild flowers picked from the roadside, and she knew he was the one.

Now she is gone, he keeps finding flower fossils pressed in books. *Encyclopaedia Britannica*, H.G. Wells's *History of Man*, dictionaries, everything. Tissue paper petals fall from the pages and he remembers what is lost.

My sister died in childbirth, and all these years I've been wondering why people I love disappear.

*

My father's absence provided the perfect conditions for gossip to flourish. There were rumours of spades knocking on wood, bashing through coffins, the covert incineration of human remains, the turning of bodies in their graves. Burial plots were proven to have been doubly sold. This was an unfortunate fact, but the question was whether the miscalculations were honest or sinister. And there was also the issue of how the previous occupants were dealt with. What alternative arrangements were made for the newly dead and improperly placed?

For a time, we were allowed to stay at the cemetery. As it was quite full, no further plots were to be re-sold. A locum cemetery manager was appointed, and he did not need to live on site.

My mother wrote to my father, sending regular updates of cemetery and church news. He replied several times, and even penned a circular to be distributed amongst those wrongly informed about the cemetery scandal. He wrote '…that I am guilty I cannot deny', but continued in other places, '…you must understand I need to clear my name. I need to be judged an innocent man.' He felt both guilty and innocent at the same time.

Now, I think I know what he was protesting against. Not that he committed a crime. He admitted to embezzling fifty-three pounds, but always reiterated the very poor state of mind he was in at the time. He also explained in the circular, of which he kept a copy, that he often borrowed money from the cemetery funds, usually to help a poor widow facing the large costs of burying her husband. The trustees were aware of this system. He merely borrowed too much this time.

Surely there is a hierarchy of sins. My father never denied that the remains of pets – fossilised cats, dogs hit by coaches, animal skeletons excavated when fresh graves were being dug, were cremated without ceremony. But his sins did not extend to disrespect for the human body, the temple, the place where the soul waits.

Or perhaps he was incapable of seeing what he had done wrong.

# 7

February 1907; it wasn't a triumphant return. Only my mother met him on the docks. She was shocked by how thin and pale he was. At least, it was a version of thinness. He was like a partly deflated balloon.

Father immediately turned himself in to the police, though he pleaded not guilty to the charge of embezzlement. A wealthy friend from church paid bail, which was also set at fifty-three pounds. And my father spent his days at home, waiting for the trial. He sipped tea from a shuddering cup, spilling it often. Lost in thought, his face turned from white, to red, to purple, then back to white again. He locked himself away in his study for hours, and returned later with his coat, hat, walking stick and a bundle of ribboned letters ready to post. He wrote so many letters – appealing for help to I'm not sure who.

The first Rex versus Truelove trial came in June. Nothing was left to the imagination. The prosecution was armed with rumours of grave-trafficking and body-burning. Even the Broadbents weren't spared. A character witness was John Broadbent, a second cousin of my mother's and stonemason at Adamant. But his reputation was shot when he was accused of trafficking just one grave. He allegedly used the profit to buy a new bicycle. It looked bad for my father, and all his supporters.

However, the defence asked the jury to take my father's philanthropic activities into account. His church work, particularly his training of boy choristers, was argued to be a testament to his sound moral character. Also, his poor mental state at the time of the crime was emphasised.

But in court, my father did not plead guilty. And even with the evidence mounted against him, the jury failed to decide on his fate.

Father endured two more trials. Finally, at the third he was found guilty and sentenced to one month's imprisonment.

While confined in gaol, my father spent his days writing letters. He wrote to a number of public figures; specifically, people he feared might have been offended by the alleged cemetery mismanagement. But he was not writing apologies. He was appealing to all the gentlemen he knew, begging to be reconsidered a worthy gentleman himself.

After a month he was released, but he remained a prisoner of his own mind. He became crazed with a need to defend his good image.

We moved across Dandenong Road to a small cottage on a property which Father had bought some years ago, before the scandal. It was just across from the cemetery, and we still played there as if it was our home. The only place we steered clear of was Adamant Monumental Works. A tall barbed wire fence enclosed it. The business had been sold to cover legal and living costs.

As soon as Father arrived home from prison, he set about directing architects on the construction of a Sculpture and Modelling School. He helped to design a grand, ornate structure – one which echoed the greatness of the real Crystal Palace and the Melbourne Exhibition Building.

Months passed. My sister and I often watched from indoors. I think we expected to see the building suddenly spring up, as instantly as Jack's beanstalk.

But one day I woke and all the sounds of sawing and hammering were gone. There was some trouble with bills. Again, Father disappeared into his study each morning, re-materialising late in the day with a coat, hat, walking stick and bundle of letters.

Christmas in 1908 was quiet. I remember hearing my parents talking softly in the kitchen. Through the keyhole, I saw him, head in his hands. She was rubbing his back. This was the first time I heard the word insolvency.

*

There was one final attempt to make everything work. The concert was organised by trustees of the Truelove Defence Fund, friends who shared a belief in my father's good name. It was to be held as soon as possible, and as the Melbourne Town Hall was unavailable at such short notice, it was held in Prahran instead.

The concert was to be an assortment of songs and recitations which would help the audience to understand the troubles at St Kilda Cemetery. My father penned a series of small stories: 'The Surprise at the Back Gate', 'Drainage Problems with Illustrations', 'The Road to Heaven – a Salvation Army Funeral', 'Cremation', 'Nursery' and 'Three Black Crows'.

A group of old chorister boys, ex-pupils of my father and now fully grown men, acted like a chorus, breaking up the spoken word with musical interludes. The evening's entertainment was essentially a dramatic and musical re-enactment of St Kilda General Cemetery's history.

My mother and some church friends made appeals at services weeks in advance, and came to the hall with impressive donations of flowers. Morning glory cuttings were draped like Christmas tinsel over the windows. Floral bunches were sold and all proceeds went to the Truelove Fund.

It was a sell-out show. Not only my father's friends came, but many eminent public figures were also in attendance. My father was not just preaching to the converted.

He was giddy by the end of the night. People crowded around, congratulating him, acknowledging his toils, offering their condolences. Many made anonymous, or not so anonymous, donations.

It was his final grand moment. The choir didn't stop singing, but performed requests late into the night. Father sang along and conducted all night. Even when mingling and chatting amongst the crowd, at least one hand continued to wave about in the air. His eyes glistened and he smiled the way I remembered as a small child.

I didn't see him collapse. There were some gasps and bustling. I looked over, and he was lying flat. My father had suffered a massive heart attack. He fell directly beneath a large painted banner. The words were sprawled across every poster and admit-one pass to the concert.

*De mortius nil nisi bonum dicendum est.*
Of the dead, speak no evil.

# 8

The ring didn't make any sense. It dropped from a velvet pouch I found tucked beneath a trove of newspaper clippings. It nearly fell between the cracks, bouncing on the splintered wooden floorboards. The sun winked at me in the golden thing.

Inside were the words 'love Charles'. And I will never be sure whether this meant from Charles, or whether it was a request.

It is three days since I buried her. She had a gold ring, identical as far as I knew, on a gold chain around her neck.

And then I found the newspaper article. The headlines read, 'Man Struck By Lightning'. I found out now that my sister was right about one thing. The man in the photograph had disappeared.

The storm came so suddenly. It was October, the middle of spring. There were four lambs. His wife and son disappeared into the farmhouse while he rounded up sheep with the dog. He did the count and saw that a lamb was missing. As it began to rain, the wife and son huddled by the stove, listening to his whistling and calls. As the thunder and lightning came closer together, they sat closer and closer to the stove, holding each other tight.

The storm passed quickly, within half an hour. The lamb was found bleating up at the farmhouse door. But the man from the photograph never came back. The soles of his unlaced boots still smoked from the sky's curse. And he became the closest thing to a holy spirit I think I know.

My mother wore the wedding ring of her first husband around her neck. Always. When she gazed at his portrait, it wasn't an invisible necklace she grasped at. It was the last little piece of what she had lost. I now believe she was the reason for his laughing eyes in the photograph. Together they shared a private joke and I'll never know what it was.

*

It's strange how often a child is close to one parent and not the other. In our family it was relatively democratic – my sister and I had one each. I grew closer to my mother. She was truth, clarity. She had that saintly quality inherited from her father, the Rechabite on a penny-farthing.

On the other hand, my father was a grey area, impossible to understand. And even after he died, my sister clung to his memory like a tear-stained pillow. They were both sucked out of existence so early, while my mother and I clung to each other in their absence.

Now, I can't understand how my mother could have hidden all these secrets from me. But it's not as though she discarded them. Perhaps she wanted me to find out the truth, but didn't know how to tell me. All these documents are so ordered, there is no way I would have failed to figure it out. It was as good as writing me a letter.

Perhaps her history was just too painful. She was twice widowed, and now it seemed she lived most of her life truly heartbroken. I never understood the way her eyes lit up when she saw my half-brother Ralph. Maybe she didn't even speak of her first husband to my sister and me because she didn't want us to feel we were born of a marriage of convenience.

I can see why we left the cemetery now. But to never speak of it again? Now I see – it was a real public scandal. We were the kids who grew up in a cemetery. If we stayed in St Kilda, or if we even told people about it, we would have been marked. Maybe she did it because she wanted more for us, a better life.

I pluck out the portrait of my father. I see at least a little more now of who he was. I will hang it above my mantelpiece, create my own little shrine. There is my father, my mother and her eyes, Grandfather Broadbent and his pointed beard, the man in the photograph – now, the man struck by lightning.

And they watch over me.

# 9

When I return to St Kilda, it is a muggy summer's day. A Salvation Army band plays Christmas carols on Chapel Street. An old man on the tuba muddles through the melody to 'Good King Wenceslas'.

Tram bells dong. Chalk arrows on the path mark the way to an All Saints' church fete, where white-haired ladies sell plum cakes, paperback novels and lemons from the rectory tree. After a short visit to the fete, I walk against the direction of the arrows and hope I'm not unknowingly defying a sign from God.

The cemetery is as it was when we left it. Almost. A petrol station now stands where the Adamant Works once stood. I'm told that the family which runs it now live at the cemetery lodge. I wonder if the children are spooked or enticed by the idea of ghosts.

I meander around the graves, the paths even more crooked than I remember. And it takes a while before I realise. I can see him here.

First it was the daisy and rose bushes, opportunistic with spaces available for growth. Fig and pear trees self-sown on the graves. A succulent with several dozen flowering pups spreads across three resting places. Two tall palm trees look borrowed from a Maui postcard. He planted seeds from all the exotic species he could find. And this is his legacy, preserved by the absence of natural predators.

He was not buried, but his ashes were interred privately. I only came to the spot once, at his funeral. I remember it well. In the Church of England section, under a great elm tree. There used to be a park bench here, before the space was required for a path. It was a favourite place for him to sit, and the small plot was reserved years ago.

There were only meant to be close friends and family at the funeral. Somehow many others found out, and it became another concert.

I sit here for a long time and let the music replay in my mind. I hum a few of his favourite tunes. I can remember the words, but I was always tone-deaf. I'm not sure why. It sounds fine inside my head, but outside it's a different story.

It seems I am imagining things when I hear the singing. It's just like I remember. The way it floated into my bedroom late at night, I'm still not sure whether the singing was real or imagined.

I jump up and try to follow the sound. But it seems to be coming from everywhere and nowhere at the same time. Or is it descending from the sky, and does this mean death is approaching? My heart is racing. I want to find out if this really is the music of ghosts.

And then I see. The carol singers are standing outside the Lodge. The door is open, a lady and her son watch. I see him mouthing the words Silent Night, Holy Night.

I didn't realise how late it is. The sky has faded from blue to purple. I never forgot the sky above the cemetery.

The mother waves and motions for me to come over. I wave back and begin to trudge towards the Lodge, humming the words under my breath.

# Notes on the Text

Charles Truelove, George Broadbent, Charles Bage and Father Gregory are all historical figures. Truelove was the manager of St Kilda General Cemetery from 1883 to 1905, and was choirmaster of All Saints' Anglican Church from 1883 to 1897.

There was a series of scandals associated with the cemetery; rumours of overcrowding, poor sanitary conditions, grave-trafficking and embezzlement. Truelove was eventually directly accused of embezzlement; he disappeared, and returned to be tried by three separate juries before being imprisoned for one month. Bail was set at fifty-three pounds, the same amount of money he had stolen.

The scandals were documented in *The Age*, *The Argus* and local St Kilda newspapers, and also in circulars, letters and flyers, a bundle of which have been preserved in a scrapbook kept by Charles Bage, a doctor who had petitioned for the closure of the cemetery. This scrapbook is kept as part of the Bage family manuscripts, and can be accessed at the State Library of Victoria. Many images and sequences of events in this story, such as the bodies turning in their graves, the image of Truelove arriving at social events in the cemetery coach, the story of the grave-robbing, have been inspired by letters, notes and accounts in various documents that I accessed in Bage's manuscripts. However, many other sequences of events and characters are entirely fictional.

Truelove did, in fact, marry George Broadbent's daughter, Marie, though I imagined the circumstances of their meeting. (Although Broadbent, allegedly, did conduct a choir of twenty-five thousand Sunday-scholars at the Exhibition Building.) They had two daughters, Winifred Ida and Kit Truelove, both of whom have many living descendants. I am one. George Broadbent is my great-great-great grandfather, Charles Truelove is my great-great grandfather, and Marie Broadbent (née Goode)

Truelove is my great-great grandmother. The unnamed protagonist of the story is fictional.

The 'choir of gravediggers' has been a key feature of my family's stories about Truelove. However, it appears that this is an invention also. In 1963, journalist and author George Blaikie published a book entitled *Scandals of Australia's Strange Past*. One chapter, titled 'Truelove in a Graveyard', told a story of how Charles Truelove led a gravedigger's choir (not called Esprit de Corpse), which increased interest in the cemetery, though also led him to mismanage funds and accidentally sell burial plots several times over.

My grandfather, Truelove's grandson, read this article and it informed (amongst his own archival research and family stories) some of his assumptions about his grandfather. In my own research, I have found no further evidence that such a choir existed. I imagined this as a significant symbolic element of my invented Charles Truelove.

My own version of Truelove's character, habits and disposition has been largely inspired by my grandfather. He was often told he was similar to Truelove in looks and nature. From my own reading about my great-great grandfather, I can also see the resemblance.

This story is a homage to my grandfather, who was intrigued by the stories surrounding Truelove. As he was dying, he said to my dad and me, 'There's a little bit of Truelove in all of us.' This story was really born from my fascination with his statement.

# Select Bibliography

## Manuscripts (held at the State Library of Victoria)

Bage family. Papers, ca. 1890–ca. 1899 [manuscript].

## Newspapers

*The Age*. South Melbourne, Victoria: Francis Cooke, 1854–.

*The Argus*. Melbourne: Argus Office, 1848–1957.

*Prahran Telegraph* (St Kilda edition). Prahran, Victoria: A.W. Osment, 1902–1920.

*St Kilda Advertiser*. Prahran, Victoria: J.H. Crabb and A. Brotherton, 1872(?)–1902.

## Secondary Sources

Blaikie, George. *Scandals of Australia's strange past*. Adelaide: Rigby, 1963.

Holden, Colin. *Saints, sinners and goalposts: a history of All Saints*. North Melbourne, Victoria: Australian Scholarly Publishing, 2008.

McLaren, Ian. *All Saints Church of England*. Melbourne: Verona Press, 1958.

Murphy, Kerry. 'Introduction: Choral Concert Life in the Late Nineteenth Century "Metropolis of the Southern Hemisphere"', *Nineteenth Century Music Review*. 2.2 (2005), xi–xiv.

Radic, Thérèse. 'Major Choral Organisations in late Nineteenth Century Melbourne', *Nineteenth Century Music Review*. 2.2 (2005), 3–28.

Soley, Stuart James. 'The highest of the high' in *'Marvellous Melbourne': All Saints' East St Kilda as Melbourne's original High Church*. East St Kilda, Victoria: All Saints Anglican Parish, 1998.

CPSIA information can be obtained
at www.ICGtesting.com
Printed in the USA
BVHW091812210822
645137BV00001B/51